For Quinn and Callan

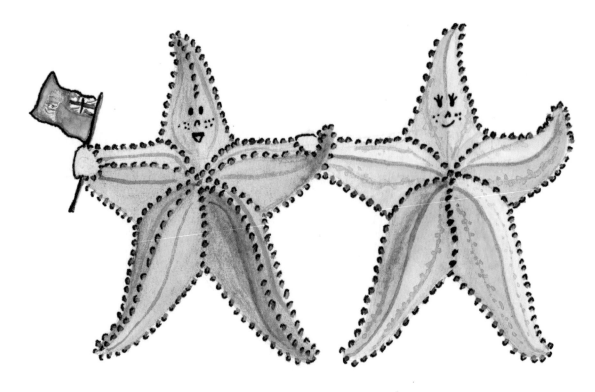

26 Sherwood Drive
PO Box 11560
Grand Cayman, KY1-1009
Cayman Islands

Published by Caribbean Creations Ltd.
ISBN 978-1-5136-0416-9
First Edition
19 18 17 16 15 / 10 9 8 7 6 5 4 3 2 1

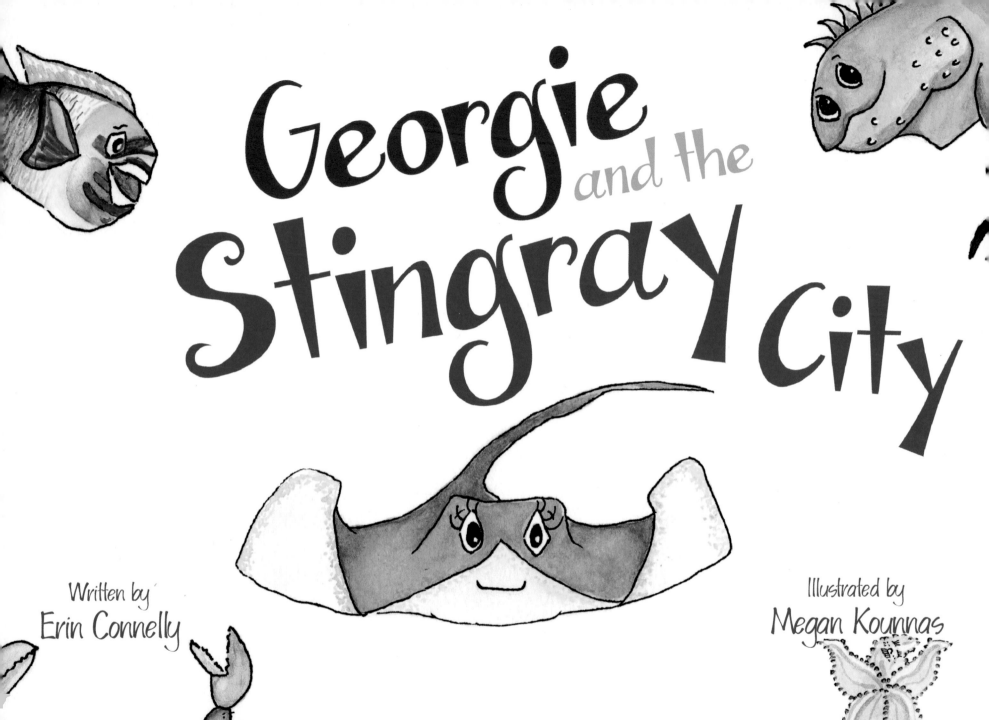

Georgie and the Stingray City

Written by
Erin Connelly

Illustrated by
Megan Kounnas

Georgie, the little stingray, floated up from the sea floor and gazed at Grand Cayman's beautiful sandy shore.

The beach stretched for miles and the water was crystal blue.

The sun was shining brightly as Georgie wondered, "What should I do?"

Just then, seven parrot fish

began darting to and fro,

exclaiming, "Hey, little stinger!

We know just where you should go!"

"It's called **STINGRAY CITY**

and it is such a cool place to play!

You'll get to see a lot of other neat places

if you go the **LONG** way."

"Oh, I'm not so sure," Georgie whispered nervously.

"It seems very far and quite a BIG swim for just little me."

"It's true. It is a long way," one of the fish said with a sigh.

"But you will never know what you can do, if you **don't at least try**."

"You're right!" said Georgie.

"I just need to believe in ME!"

And with that she thanked the kind fish

and set off through the calm blue sea.

Soon Georgie came upon a lovely cove she had never been to before.

It was covered in white sand and a little crab stood on the shore.

"Good day, I'm Mr. Smith," said the crab, "How do you do?

I bet you're looking for a city filled with creatures just like you!"

"Yes, yes I am!" Georgie bubbled with glee.

"Would you be so kind and give directions to me?"

"Well of course," said Mr. Smith, "I'm always happy to lend a claw.

Just keep swimming until you see a castle sitting near the iron wall."

"Thank you so much!" shouted Georgie,

as she went on her way,

excited about the next place

she would get to explore today.

Then in the distance Georgie saw a blue spiky fellow.

He was sunning himself on some rocks and looking quite mellow.

"Excuse me, Mr. Iguana, am I going the right way?

I am looking for the sandbar city, home of the stingray."

"No problem, mon, and James is my name.

You still have a bit farther, but you will be so glad you came.

Just keep heading East until you get to the End.

Then turn to the left and go around the bend.

When you get to the Point you will almost be there.

I know you CAN do it! Goodbye and take care!"

So Georgie started swimming just as fast as she could go,

and soon swam right past some rocks putting on a spectacular show.

It was a gigantic fountain blowing the sea up to the sky.

Georgie stared in awe as she had never seen water fly so high.

Georgie knew she just needed to keep following the ironshore,
but she was getting so tired and wasn't sure if she could swim anymore.

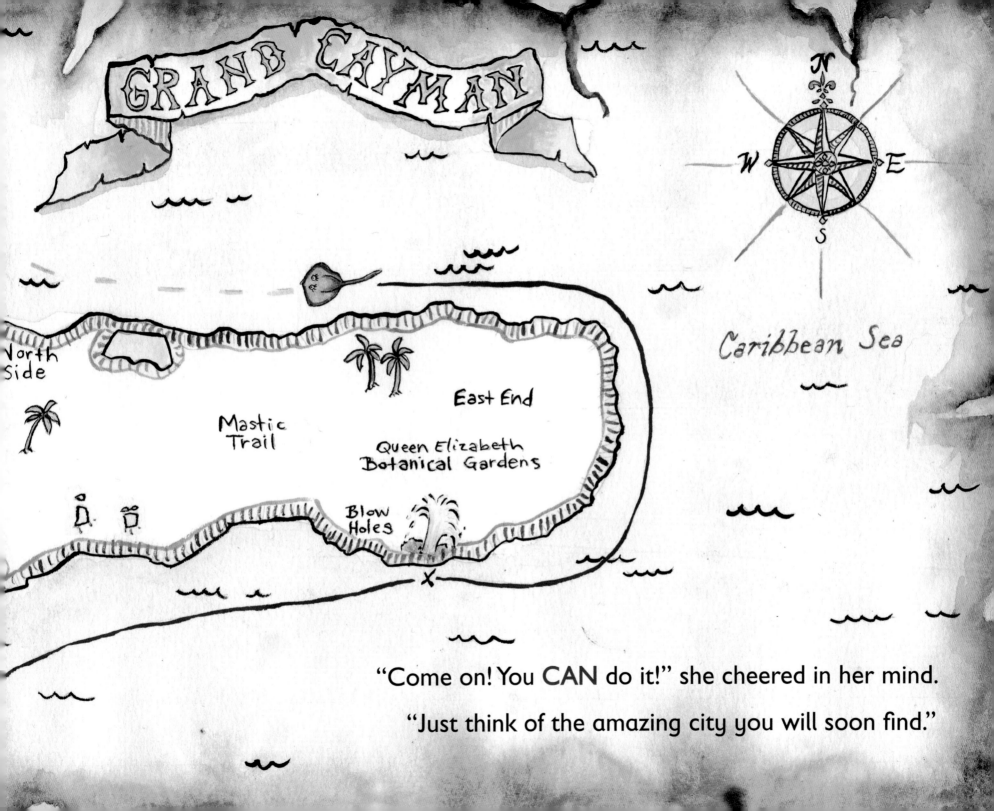

GRAND CAYMAN

N
W E
S

Caribbean Sea

North Side

Mastic Trail

East End

Queen Elizabeth Botanical Gardens

Blow Holes

X

"Come on! You **CAN** do it!" she cheered in her mind.

"Just think of the amazing city you will soon find."

Then through the clear water she saw the Point on the land

and two little starfish having fun in the sand.

The two tiny friends,

  named Rummy and Kai,

waved hello to the little stingray

  as she went passing by.

Georgie swam out to the North but did not hear a Sound.

She began losing hope that her destination would ever be found.

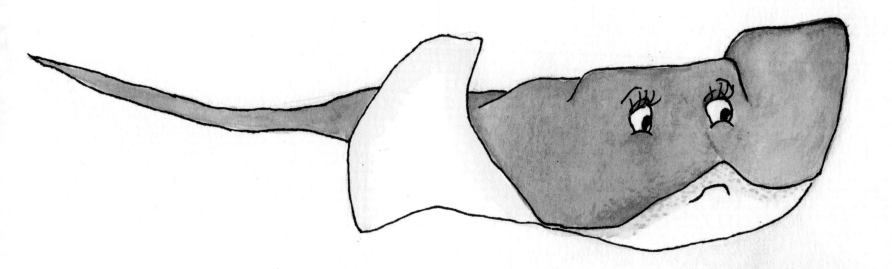

But then, all of a sudden,

Georgie saw the most amazing sight!

A sandbar full of stingrays

gliding through the water with such delight!

It was like a huge party under the sun.

Even a couple of seagulls swooped down to join in the FUN.

Georgie smiled with pride as she looked at the city.

"I am so glad I tried, as missing this would be quite a pity!"

So with just a little courage and some help from new friends,

Georgie made it to STINGRAY CITY where this adventure ends.

Then with a swish of her stinger, off swam the little ray,

to have some more fun and enjoy the rest of her beautiful Caribbean day.

National Flag

George Town
Capital City

Silver Thatch Palm
National Tree

Little Cayman

Cayman Brac

Grand Cayman

Wild Banana Orchid
National Flower

Cayman
Fun Facts